Shapesh

Pratima Mitchell

Illustrated by
Chris Coady
Cassandre Maxwell
Yannick Roberts
Aleks Sennwald

CONTENTS

OXFORD
UNIVERSITY PRESS

Dear Reader,

Shapeshifter stories are found in almost every culture in the world. The idea of shapeshifting is a gift to storytellers. It can be used in so many different ways, for example to punish or reward characters, to rescue or endanger them, or simply to open their eyes to the magic that lies under the surface of everyday life.

I enjoyed reading dozens of tales from all over the world to make up this collection of shapeshifter stories. I even asked friends to remember tales they had heard as children. Like all storytellers, I sometimes changed the details to make them more exciting and suitable for my audience (you).

After each story, think about what effect the shapeshifting had on the characters. Did it leave you feeling relieved, or sad? Did you smile, or did you feel uneasy?

Perhaps you might want to write a shapeshifter story yourself …

Pratima Mitchell

The Flowering Tree

A folk tale from Southern India

Chapter 1

The gift

Sonu and Munni were two sisters who lived in the southern Indian town of Mysore. Sonu was twelve and Munni was sixteen. Many rich people lived in Mysore in big houses with gardens. They had servants to cook and clean for them. The rich never had to worry about food or clothes.

There were also many poor people in Mysore. The poor people worked very hard just to make enough money for one meal a day.

Sonu and Munni's father died when they were little. Their widowed mother slaved away, day and night, to earn enough money for them to live. She had three cleaning jobs. With the money she earned she was able to pay for her girls to go to school.

• *Sonu:* (say) 'soh-noo'.   • *Munni:* (say) 'mun-nee'.
• *Mysore:* (say) 'my-saw'.

3

Sonu and Munni had only two dresses each. They wore one and washed the other so it was clean for the next day. They didn't have money for shoes, but they always looked neat and tidy. Life was hard, but they had one another.

'Let's sweep the yard today,' Munni told her younger sister. Munni knew that her mother's life was hard. 'Poor Amma looks so tired. Can you see the shadows under her eyes?'

'You sweep and I'll wash the rice and pick the stones out of the lentils,' said Sonu. 'That will save Amma a lot of time and she can put her feet up when she comes home.'

'She loves it when I rub her feet with coconut oil. I'll also massage her poor tired arms,' added Munni.

The girls loved their mother and they worried about her health.

'It would be good to celebrate Diwali properly,' sighed Munni. 'If only we had a hundred rupees! What would you buy?'

Sonu thought for a few minutes. 'Green bangles for Amma, oil for Diwali lights and a box of almond sweets.'

'I'd buy her a necklace of pearls and some sparklers to set off on Diwali night,' said Munni.

* * *

The next day, as the girls were walking home from school, an old beggar woman held out her begging bowl. The girls shook their heads sadly. 'We're sorry, but we ourselves are so poor that we can't help you.'

'Give me something ... anything ... I'll exchange it for a green coconut to quench my thirst,' begged the old lady. She looked so old and sad that Munni pulled out the red ribbon in her hair. 'There, granny,' she said. 'Take my ribbon and buy a coconut.'

'Ram Ram,' the girls chorused, blessing the
old lady, as they walked on.

'Wait a minute!' the old woman cried.
She hobbled after them. 'You have shown
real kindness even though you have so little
yourselves. In return, I will give you a gift so
you will never be poor again.' She whispered
something in Munni's ear. 'If you do exactly
what I say, you'll always have money.' Then she
disappeared down a dark lane.

Chapter 2
Selling flowers

The sisters came home bubbling over with excitement. Sonu fetched a bucket of water and Munni stood in the yard before the great tree that grew there. Then both girls bowed deeply towards it. Sonu said the magic spell that the old lady had whispered to them. Munni held out her arms and Sonu carefully splashed her sister with water from the bucket. She splashed her head down to her feet. She splashed water on her arms and hands, her neck, her face, her head and her hair. Then she splashed every inch of Munni's back. The air is tropical and warm in Mysore, so Munni enjoyed the feel of the cool water on her body.

Then Sonu watched in amazement as Munni's legs and feet slowly turned hard and dark brown. They started to look like a tree trunk. Her arms turned into branches. Her fingers became twigs and shiny green leaves began to sprout all over

her arms and fingers. Next, tiny buds appeared and opened into beautiful waxy white flowers.

With nimble fingers, Sonu gathered the flowers into a basket. She was careful not to break a twig or hurt the tree in any way. When all the flowers had been plucked, Sonu sprinkled every part of the tree with water. She drew a

breath of relief when she saw Munni standing before her once more. The girls hugged one another and jumped up and down with joy. They planned to take the basket of flowers to the King's palace. They were sure the Queen would pay them well for the flowers. Then they would have enough money for Diwali presents for their mother.

First they wove the delicate flowers into garlands. 'The Queen can put them around the statues of gods and goddesses in the palace temple,' Sonu said. She looked more closely at a white flower. It was small and shaped like a trumpet. Its centre was a rosy pink and the underside of each petal was a pale yellowy-green. It was perfect. Its perfume was a glorious mix of gardenia, rose, jasmine and lemon.

Sure enough when the sisters called out their wares near the palace gates, the Queen's maid ran out. She bought the whole basket of flowers. The Queen was so delighted with them that she sent her maid after the girls.

'Her Majesty asks if you will bring these garlands every morning for her temple. She wants to know where you got these lovely flowers.' The girls thanked the maid but would not tell her where the flowers were from.

* * *

Every morning for a whole week, Sonu and Munni waited until their mother had gone to work. Then they performed the water splashing ceremony, never forgetting to bow to the tree in the yard first. Sonu was always careful that every part of her sister's body was wet. After gently plucking the flowers, she would splash Munni with water again. Then they both picked up their school bags and went to the palace to sell the basket of flowers.

After a week, the girls counted their money. There was enough for their mother's Diwali presents. On Diwali night they filled little clay lamps with oil. They lit the cotton wicks and placed the lamps all over the house and yard.

'Goddess Lakshmi will come and bless our home. She will be able to see her way to our house and bring wealth and good luck,' said Munni.

Sonu and Munni gave their mother her presents. When she saw the pearl necklace, the green bangles and the box of expensive almond sweets, she started to cry.

'Why are you so sad dear Amma? Don't you like our gifts? Look, here are some sparklers to frighten away the demons! And Lakshmi will come and visit us now.'

Their mother wiped away her tears. 'I am so happy that I can't quite believe what I see. But I am also sad because I am afraid.'

'Afraid of what, dear Amma?' Sonu asked.

'Afraid that you may have done something wicked to be able to buy all this.'

'Never, Amma, never,' said Munni. She pressed her mother's tired feet. 'I will tell you how we earned this money.' And she told her mother the story of the old beggar lady and the great gift that she had given to the sisters.

Chapter 3
The Prince

The two sisters continued to earn extra money until, one day, the Queen's younger son noticed the beautiful white flowers.

'What is this species of jasmine?' he wondered. 'Neither a true jasmine, nor a gardenia, nor any blossom that I can identify.' The Prince was a curious young man. He was also studying the science of plants. So he sent for the greatest botanists in the country to help him identify the flower.

Not one had the slightest idea what it was or where it came from. So the young Prince decided to find out for himself. He watched the girls who brought the basket of flowers each morning to the palace gates.

He noticed that the older girl, Munni, was a very pretty young woman. She had a long braid of shining black hair. Carefully woven into the braid were the white flowers. The scent of them was enough to make him feel he was in paradise.

The Prince looked into her big black eyes and fell in love with her.

Munni was shy. When the Prince spoke to her and asked about the flowers she stuttered and blushed and looked at the ground. But she would not give him the information he so desperately wanted. She said vaguely that she knew a shrub that grew in the hills behind Mysore. Yes, it flowered all year round. No, it didn't have a name.

The Prince found it a very odd story. He made up his mind to secretly watch the sisters so that he could find out more about the lovely white flowers.

The next day, the Prince got up at the crack of dawn and arrived at Sonu and Munni's house. He hid behind some bushes and waited for them to come out to do their chores. He saw Sonu draw water from the well and then watched Munni changing from her human form. He saw how gently and carefully her sister picked the beautiful, fragrant flowers. He breathed a sigh of relief when Munni became a girl again.

Then he went back to the palace and asked to

see his mother, the Queen.

'Mother, I have fallen in love with a beautiful flower seller. I want to marry her and make her my princess.'

At first his mother was astonished. Then she looked out of her window and saw pretty young Munni, so she sent for the girl's mother.

Munni's mother was surprised by the Prince's wishes, but seeing that Munni was in love too, she agreed to the marriage.

'I will worry about you all the time,' she told her older daughter. 'You are a clever girl but how will you cope with royal ways and palace gossip? You must promise to come home again if you are ever unhappy.'

Munni reassured her mother as best she could. Sonu was delighted for her sister.

'You see, it's true, Amma,' Sonu said. 'Goddess Lakshmi has come to our house – just like we said she would!'

Chapter 4
Jealousy

The young Prince was very romantic. He believed he had rescued Munni from a life of poverty. But he didn't know her at all, and didn't know what to talk about on their wedding night.

'Show me where you get the flowers from,' he asked innocently. 'I want to pick them and decorate our room with them.'

Munni explained what happened when her sister sprinkled a bucket of water on her and taught him the spell. The Prince asked his servant to bring water to his rooms. He gently began to water his tree-bride and soon he saw the flowering tree appear in place of the girl he had just married.

He picked the delicate white flowers and strew them on the floor. Their heavenly smell perfumed the air. Then he brought Munni back to her own self. It broke the ice and they started talking and getting to know each other.

* * *

The Prince had a younger sister who was jealous of Munni. Before he married, the Prince had given his sister all his attention. Now that Munni was the light of his life his sister could not bear it.

'Mother,' she complained to the Queen soon after, 'why do my brother and his new wife throw out heaps of flowers every day? A mountain of dead petals is growing outside their room!'

The Queen hushed her daughter. She was just glad that her son and his new wife seemed so happy. But the Princess was determined to find out where the white flowers came from.

That night she put her eye to the keyhole and saw how her brother helped Munni to become a tree. She saw him pick the flowers.

She saw him scatter them all over the floor
and furniture, and she smelled the heavenly scent
which wafted through the cracks in the door.

A few days later the Princess invited Munni to come with her to the palace gardens. As the Princess took a turn on the swing, she looked slyly at her sister-in-law. 'I know all about the flowers. I know your secret! I saw my brother

washing you with water and how you have the power to change yourself into a flowering tree! Now you must let me do the same with you.'

Munni wanted to scold the Princess for spying and tell her she had no right to make demands on her. But Munni was a newcomer to the royal household. She was afraid to disagree and to say what she really felt. So she agreed to teach the Princess the words of the spell. It was a bad mistake.

The Princess splashed water on Munni but as soon as Munni became a tree, she tore off the flowers and snapped the branches and twigs. Then she became tired of the game and roughly threw some water on the tree, not caring where it fell.

Munni was unable to come back to life because some parts of her were still dry and some of her branches were broken. She was left in the garden in a terrible state. She lay by the swings helplessly until the gardeners carried her away and threw her on a rubbish heap.

Chapter 5
Rescue

By evening Munni had not come back to her prince. She was lying on the garden rubbish moaning softly and in great pain. The Prince searched all over Mysore looking for his new wife. He went to her old home, but she wasn't there. Nor could he find her in the temple, or the market place. He asked Sonu to join him on his search and they looked high and low without success.

The Prince did not sleep all night. He missed Munni desperately and he wept, thinking he might never see her again.

Next morning he looked out of the window of their apartment in the palace and saw the gardeners carrying the prunings and rubbish from the garden to be burned. One of them was dragging a small tree. The Prince shouted, 'Stop! Wait!'

He ran downstairs and looked closely at

the tree. He thought he recognised the pattern in the bark and the shiny green leaves, which were starting to fade. He thought he heard a faint moan and he pulled the tree away from the gardener and carried it to his room. He wept to see its sorry state, its broken branches and splintered twigs. Surely this was his Munni!

Fetching a bucket of water he began to tenderly bathe the tree, all the time singing, 'Come back Munni, come back to me.' He sponged every bit of the bark and every leaf until he felt the tree coming back to life.

He carried on patiently until his young wife's face appeared and then her long black hair, all tangled and dusty. Then her neck and body and arms emerged and finally her legs and feet. Munni stood before him, looking tired but whole again. They embraced and murmured how much they loved one another.

'Please don't change me into a flowering tree again,' Munni said to her prince.

The Prince wrote the words of the spell on

a piece of paper – the same spell that the old beggar woman had taught the sisters many months ago. He struck a match and held it to the paper. The paper caught fire and was soon a heap of ashes.

'That was then, and this is now,' declared the Prince, and he and Munni lived happily ever after.

Eglé

A folk tale from Lithuania

Chapter 1

The deal

In the hot summer months, there was nothing more refreshing than spending time at the river. Eglé and her two sisters spent their mornings swimming, washing their hair and basking in the shade of a willow tree.

One fine day, with a deep blue sky above and a crowd of yellow and red butterflies dancing on the riverbank, Eglé came out of the water to dry herself. She wrung her beautiful long black hair and wiped the water from her face, arms and legs. She turned to pick up her blouse and skirt. But what she saw in front of her sent the blood racing in her veins.

'Help, sisters, help!' she shouted.

Her two sisters waded out of the water and ran to find Eglé trembling with fear. She was as white as a sheet. Too frightened to speak, Eglé pointed to her blouse and skirt. In front of them, barring her way, was a writhing mass of snakes!

The snakes twisted, hissed and flicked their red tongues. They were like blue-black eels and more than twelve centimetres long. One of them fixed his small shining eyes on Eglé and spoke. 'Come with me Eglé and marry me. I will make you very happy. You will have everything you could want from life.'

Eglé was shocked to hear the snake speak. She was even more shocked at his suggestion and shook with revulsion. 'Please, just let me have my clothes and let me go home to my parents. You can have whatever else you want.'

'Ah, but the only thing I want is you, Eglé!' said the snake. His companions wriggled and writhed and slithered and coiled themselves in and out of one another.

Eglé and her sisters were afraid of the snakes. But they were also afraid of the trouble they would get into if they went home without all their clothes. They were from the royal family, so they were expected to be well-dressed and dignified at all times.

The snake slithered closer to the girls. His tongue flicked like a dangerous spark in and out of his mouth. Eglé trembled. She was desperate to get away.

'All right,' she said. 'Give me my clothes and let me go home now. But tomorrow, I'll go with you.'

The three sisters ran all the way home. They told their parents, the King and Queen, about their strange meeting with the snakes on the riverbank.

When their brothers heard what happened they were angry and shook their fists. 'It's the Snake King! We know him. We'll be only too glad to teach him a lesson.' They reached for their weapons.

'Wait!' commanded the King. 'There is another way.'

He turned to his wife, the Queen. 'My dear,' he said, 'with your help we can fob him off with something else. After all, a snake won't be able to tell the difference between our daughter and some other creature.' His eyes twinkled and the royal family laughed.

Chapter 2
The tricks

Next morning, a whole embassy of snakes arrived at court. They slithered and wriggled up the steps to the throne room.

The Minister of Foreign Affairs spoke coldly to them. 'Here is the fulfilment of Princess Eglé's promise to your Snake King. Please leave now and don't return.' The Minister handed over a white duck that the Queen had dressed in Eglé's blue bonnet.

The duck was terrified of the slimy creatures and went off squawking and protesting.

The next morning the snakes were back, hissing angrily. 'Our King does not like being bamboozled! A duck indeed! Hand us over Princess Eglé, or else!'

Eglé's brothers were ready to kill the snakes, but they were stopped by their mother.

This time the snakes were given a white goat dressed in Eglé's pink and yellow shawl.

The poor goat went off bleating in a piteous way.

But next morning the snakes came back. And they came back in greater numbers than before. This time they threatened to invade the palace if Eglé's promise was not honoured.

When Eglé saw thousands of snakes swarming up the palace steps she decided that she could no longer avoid her pledge. She packed her clothes and with many unhappy tears left her mother, father, sisters and brothers. She went with the snakes to their kingdom under the sea.

Chapter 3
A new life

When Eglé reached the sea
bed, the most handsome
man she had ever seen
came up to her. He took
her hand and kissed it.
'Welcome to my kingdom
under the sea, Eglé. I am
Zilvinas, the Snake King.
I will always take care of you
and do my best to make you happy.'

The palace was built of red coral and full of
beautiful furniture and pictures. Eglé resigned
herself to her fate. She tried not to think of the
past, but to enjoy the present. In time, the Snake
King and Eglé had four children, three boys and
a girl. They were a happy and devoted family.

Eglé had almost forgotten her past life,
but one day the children asked her about
their relations.

'Don't we have any uncles, aunts and cousins? And what about your parents, Mother? We would love to visit your parents and your childhood home.'

Now Zilvinas was devoted to his children and he couldn't bear to see them restless and forever wanting to know about his wife. He was sad to see Eglé downcast, as she thought about the life she had left behind.

One morning, Eglé came to Zilvinas. 'Please let me go back to my parents for a holiday,' she begged him. 'The children need to meet their grandparents. By now my sisters must have married and may have children of their own!'

Zilvinas was torn. He loved his wife and he was frightened of losing her. But he also knew how much a visit would mean to her. After some thought, Zilvinas gave her a fortnight to visit her family, on condition that she fulfil three tasks.

'Show me that you can spin thread from this ball of red silk. Then wear down these iron clogs and lastly bake a cake to take home.'

To her great dismay, Eglé found that the ball of silk kept producing more and more thread. She spun and spun and it wouldn't come to an end. Finally she asked a wise old woman for advice.

The old woman told her to throw the ball in the fire. When she did, out jumped a frog, and sure enough, the thread stopped coming. The frog had been producing the never-ending silk from its mouth.

Next, the old woman advised Eglé to take the iron clogs to the blacksmith. The blacksmith soon hammered them down with his tools.

The last task was almost impossible. Zilvinas had destroyed all the baking dishes. Only a sieve was left. The wise old woman showed Eglé how to patch it up with clay, and joyfully Eglé produced a superb cake to take to her family.

Zilvinas knew he had to honour his promise. He said goodbye to his family with a heavy heart. 'Come back soon. If you need me, then come to the seashore and sing:

'Zilvinas, dear Zilvinas, if alive may the sea foam milk,

If dead may the sea foam blood, Zilvinas, dear Zilvinas!'

Chapter 4
Betrayal

For the next two weeks Eglé and her children had the most wonderful holiday with her family. They went on picnics, they swam in the river, they told stories and ate delicious food.

Eglé's brothers said to her, 'Stay here. Don't go back. We love you and your children and cannot bear the thought of losing you again.'

Eglé smiled but shook her head. 'I love my husband and the ways of the undersea kingdom. I can't stay.'

But the brothers became angry. They were determined to make her stay. They plotted to kill Zilvinas if only they could get him to come out of the sea.

First they asked Eglé's sons to call their father, but the boys refused. Then the uncles started to work on their niece. 'Tell us how we can summon your father. We want to thank him and embrace him.'

The little girl innocently took her uncles down to the shore and called:

'Zilvinas, dear Zilvinas, if alive may the sea foam milk,

If dead may the sea foam blood, Zilvinas dear Zilvinas!'

Immediately, her father rose from the sea in a great rush of bubbles and foam. Eglé's brothers rushed to him with spears and swords and killed him. They threw his body back into the sea and returned to their palace.

When Eglé saw her daughter sobbing and her brothers looking pleased with themselves, a terrible fear crept into her heart. 'What have you done?' she screamed at her brothers. Their silence frightened her even more.

Eglé ran down to the seashore and called her husband. The sea started to foam dark red and she knew her beloved was dead.

Eglé cursed her brothers. 'I can never be happy in your house,' she cried. 'You have betrayed my trust in you. You may as well have killed me too.'

Then in her anger and grief she turned to her daughter. 'And as for you, you have betrayed your father. I am going to turn you into an aspen tree. You will always tremble whenever the breeze blows.' And Eglé did just that. Her daughter became a slender aspen, with leaves that quiver and shiver with the slightest breath of wind.

As for Eglé herself, she could not bear to look at her brothers ever again. She was determined not to share her family with them. So, with great sadness, she changed her sons into oak trees and herself into a tall and upright spruce tree. Her brothers knew they had done wrong, but nothing could bring back Eglé. Love and jealousy had killed her.

The Demon Fox

A folk tale from Korea

Chapter 1
The answer to a prayer

In the depths of the Korean countryside lived a farmer and his wife who had three sons but no daughter. They would often pray to the mountain spirits to bless them with a girl. The farmer's wife longed for a daughter – she wanted to dress a little girl in pretty things and to braid her hair. She wanted to teach her to sew and cook and share the special love between mother and daughter.

One day the farmer's wife was so desperate in her longing that when night fell her husband made his way to a famous shrine.

He stood before the shrine, closed his eyes and folded his hands in prayer, 'Please, please give us a girl. We will love and cherish her with all our hearts, whatever her faults.'

Soon his wife became pregnant and in due course had the sweetest-looking girl you had ever seen. The baby had fine hair and fair skin. Her eyes were a reddish brown and her hands and feet were narrow but strong. Her parents were delighted and called the baby girl Yoora.

When Yoora reached the age of six she was given her own room to sleep in. She was a playful and clever child and kept her mother busy and amused. However, at this time the farmer noticed that one by one his cows were mysteriously dying. He called his oldest son, Seung, and asked him to keep a watch on the cowshed. On the night of the full moon Seung saw a dreadful sight …

• *Seung:* (say) 'soong'.

The next day, his father asked if anything unusual had taken place at night. Seung hesitated, then said that he had seen Yoora putting a deathly curse on the cow.

'What lies and nonsense you are talking!' The old man gave Seung a cuff round the ears. 'Go away and don't ever come back to this house. You are just jealous of Yoora and want me to give you her inheritance.' The farmer was outraged to think that his son was lying. He also knew how his wife doted on the girl. It would have broken her heart to hear anything against her sweet little daughter.

Poor Seung left the farmhouse in disgrace. But the cows kept dying. So the old farmer asked the middle son, Jung Hee, to keep watch on them.

All went well for a few weeks until the night of the full moon. This time their favourite brown cow was found dead in the morning. Jung Hee told his father what had happened. 'I could not believe my eyes, respected Father!'

• *Jung Hee:* (say) 'jung-he'.   **49**

'At midnight I heard my sister get up. She went to the cowshed. She put a deathly curse on the cow. I was terribly frightened, Father, please believe what I say.'

However, his father also dismissed his story with angry words. 'You too are a liar and are no longer my son. Get out of this house now and never come back!'

Jung Hee left the home that he loved, just as his older brother had done before him.

The two brothers were penniless and had only the clothes on their backs. They wandered around the countryside together like beggars. They walked from shrine to shrine until they came to a Buddhist temple. There they met a monk who kindly let them stay.

Chapter 2
The brothers

Back at the farmhouse, the youngest brother, Kwan, played his cards very cleverly. He saw what had happened to his two older brothers. When his father asked him to keep watch on the cows, to try to find out why they were dying, he was determined not to follow the fate of his brothers.

On the night of the full moon, Kwan saw his sister cursing one of the cows; then he saw her wash her hands and face in the stream and creep back to bed. In the morning, when his father questioned him he said he had seen nothing unusual.

'I think that the full moon has an effect on animals. Perhaps the cows were frightened when they saw the bright face of the moon.

'Whatever happened, it was certainly not our sister Yoora.'

The farmer put his hand on Kwan's head. He blessed him. 'You are a very good son. I shall leave half my wealth to you and half to Yoora.'

* * *

Some years later, Seung and Jung Hee started to feel homesick. They missed their mother and father and they missed the farm. There was never enough to eat in the monastery and they had to beg for their bowl of rice from strangers. They decided to return home.

Before they left, the old monk gave them three bottles – a red, a blue and a white one. 'You will need these, I think. From what you have told me, I think your sister Yoora is probably a demon fox. If she tries to harm you, throw one of these at her.'

The brothers bowed to the monk and started home.

The journey took Seung and Jung Hee three days and nights. They trekked over blue mountains and through white rivers. They fought off bears and tigers and crossed a wide lake.

Finally they arrived back in familiar countryside. They rejoiced to see the blossom on the trees and to hear the sound of the birds they knew. But as soon as they came to their own fields, they looked at one another with alarm.

Something was wrong.

There were no crops to admire. The outhouses were neglected and broken and they could hear no birds singing. The roof of the farmhouse was falling down. The courtyard was thick with thorns and weeds.

They called and called for their father and
mother, but no one answered. They called for
Kwan and no answer came. They made their
way inside the house. There, crouching in the
kitchen, was Yoora. She greeted them with a
wide smile, but they saw that her teeth had
become very sharp and pointed. They were filled
with dread. Even the family dogs cowered
before her.

Chapter 3
The feast

'Come brothers,' said Yoora. 'It's so good to see you. Please come and eat with me. I will cook a delicious feast.'

Seung and Jung Hee were frightened and said they would not stay. They didn't question Yoora about their parents or Kwan. They knew they wouldn't hear the truth from her.

'You can't travel on this cold night,' she said. 'Look, the moon is rising, and tonight is a full moon. Ghosts and demons will trip you up, owls and bats will fly into your hair. Come, stay just this night and keep me company.'

The brothers looked at one another. It was difficult to refuse her now. With great reluctance they made their beds in a corner while she prepared a scrumptious feast for them.

They all ate and drank heartily. Seung and
Jung Hee licked their fingers and asked for more,
because they had been so hungry during their
years in the monastery. Finally, they went to
sleep, but they still felt uneasy.

* * *

In the middle of the night, Seung woke up
suddenly. He could hear something strange. He lit
a candle and saw Yoora, wide awake, in the middle
of the room. The noise of her chewing had woken
him. She was eating the leftovers but in a way that
made him shudder. Yoora's eyes were as wild and
strange as an animal feasting on its prey.

Then he noticed that she held a sharp knife in her hand. She slowly raised it above the sleeping Jung Hee. With a terrible cry, Seung leapt out of bed, dragged his brother to his feet and shouted, 'Run, run away from this house of death!'

But there was no escape. Yoora ran after them and just when she was nearly at their side, Seung remembered the small bottles in his pocket. He threw the red bottle and immediately a wall of smoke went up between the brothers and their demon sister. A thicket of thorns rose up and made a barrier. But Yoora changed herself into a red fox and scrambled through the thorn bushes, charging after them with her long tail flying behind.

The demon fox was soon at the brothers' heels again. In desperation, Seung threw the blue bottle at the fox. This time a large lake sprang into existence. The water lapped the shores and the wind whipped up the waves. But this was no problem for the fox. The creature swam and paddled through at lightning speed and soon caught up with the brothers once again, as they were beginning to tire.

Seung had one last chance. His final weapon was the white bottle. He threw it behind him and a fierce fire leapt up from the ground.

This time the fox demon could not escape. She was running too quickly to stop, so with a final piercing scream she was swallowed up into the roaring flames.

The brothers stopped, panting and exhausted. The brothers' hearts kept on pounding until they were sure that the demon fox was nothing but cinders.

Out of the smoke flew a tiny insect. The mosquito furiously buzzed around Seung's head. He swatted it easily. That was the very end of the demon fox.

And that is why, even to this day, the fox and the mosquito are both afraid of fire.

The Leopard and Her Cubs

A legend from the Great Rift Valley, Africa

Chapter 1

Mukanda

Many years ago, in a clearing in the Great Rift Valley, lived a tribe of hunters and gatherers. Their village was next to a dark and mysterious forest. The men hunted wild animals and collected honey. The women gathered fruit; they picked leaves to boil for vegetables and dug up roots that made a tasty meal.

Both men and women painted their bodies with clay and lime. The women worked hard all day, but looked beautiful with decorations of beads and flowers. The men were strong and brave. Among them, the bravest of the hunters was Mukanda.

No challenge was too much for Mukanda. He could outrun the fastest man. He could track a cheetah or a leopard, a lion or a wildebeest. He could swing a hyena by its tail and send it to the moon. He swam like a fish in Lake Nakuru and dodged the wild elephants when they charged.

When he went hunting for food he always brought back a sackful of game to his village for skinning.

It seemed that Mukanda was born to set himself impossible tasks. When he hunted, he went into the most dangerous parts of the forest. Since he didn't know the meaning of fear, he performed feats which none of the other hunters would even dream of doing. He would track man-eating lions all alone, plunge into rapids to get the biggest catch of fish; he would chase antelope for three days at a time and climb the tallest tree in the forest in order to snatch a huge beehive hanging from the top branch.

Normally, the people in the village married among themselves. But Mukanda was different. He sent a message to neighbouring villages that he was looking for a beautiful girl to marry and have his children.

After all, he was the bravest and strongest man for miles around. He wanted a partner who was also extraordinary!

Chapter 2
The hunt

Some time later, the headman from a far-off
tribe came with many gifts and the offer of his
daughter's hand in marriage. She was unusually
beautiful and clever and brought with her a
big dowry.

Mukanda was delighted. After they were
married his wife soon became pregnant.
Mukanda was sure that the child would be a boy.
He wanted his son to become an even greater
hunter than he was. So, he started thinking of
ways to make sure that it happened. The child
would have the best food, the best training,
the best companions – in fact, the very best

of everything!

Mukanda consulted the village wise man, the witch doctor. The wise man told him that there was indeed a secret way to make his son grow into a superb hunter.

He must provide two leopard skins for the baby to sleep on, and they had to be the skins of two very young leopard cubs.

That was no problem for Mukanda. He prepared to go on a solo hunting trip to look for leopard cubs.

Mukanda took his bow and arrows, his axe and his hunting knife. He asked his wife to grease him with the fat of a gazelle, because he would have to run fast. Then he set off for the dark forest.

On the way he met snakes and scorpions. He was ambushed by yellow monkeys, he fended off a panther and killed a mad elephant. At last he found what he was looking for – two beautiful leopard cubs sleeping against the roots of a baobab tree.

The cubs were nestled against one another like yellow catkins. Their underbellies were creamy white and their fur was softer than down. With an inward shout of triumph, Mukanda snatched them up and put them in his bag of hide.

He ran home as fast as his legs would carry him, leaping and singing for joy. Mukanda planned to spread the skins under his baby son at the naming ceremony. He hoped that his son would absorb some of the magic energy and power of leopards. Then his boy would grow to become the best hunter that Kenya had ever known.

Mukanda was very happy when, a few days later, his wife gave birth. The baby was a boy.

Chapter 3
Revenge

Meanwhile the leopard mother came back from her hunt and was shocked to find her cubs missing. She searched round and round the baobab tree. She went trotting all over the dark forest and cried for her little ones to mew and show her where they were hiding.

She was almost mad with grief. By nightfall the leopard mother realised that her cubs had been stolen. With tears rolling down her face, she started to look for clues to find who had taken them.

Keeping her nose to the ground, she sniffed and sought out any tell-tale smells. She caught a whiff of the hunter's recent presence, and then his flight from the forest.

She followed the trail, and as she followed it her appearance started to change. First her

face became a human face – that of a woman;
her limbs changed to human arms and she grew a
human torso. Her spots disappeared and her skin
became smooth and black. Finally, her entire
shape changed into that of a beautiful woman.

Tall and lithe, the leopard woman quickly
loped through the forest and came to Mukanda's
village. It was getting dark, but the trail of scent
led her to Mukanda's sleeping hut.

She greeted Mukanda and said she was lost. She asked if she could stay the night. Enchanted by her beauty, Mukanda agreed.

The leopard woman watched Mukanda preparing for the naming ceremony of his son. There were several rituals to complete before the morning, and he explained what he was doing.

'I have to sacrifice the two baby leopards. I shall skin them and cure them. They will become my son's mattress.'

At this the stranger began to cry. 'Oh please don't do that, good sir. Have pity on the babies. They are so beautiful and their mother will miss them so much!' She sobbed and pleaded with Mukanda.

Mukanda just laughed.

She begged him once more, but he continued to laugh, throwing back his brave head and showing his white teeth.

When she heard him laughing in this careless way, the leopard woman's beautiful form shook with anger and pain.

Her body started to change. Mukanda stopped laughing and stared at her.

She seemed to be melting into another shape – slowly, slowly – her arms extended into legs, her fingers flexed into claws, her face became cat-like, and sharp teeth glistened in her mouth. She was transforming into a leopard!

With a terrible roar the leopard mother sprang at Mukanda and threw him to one side of the hut.

When she was finished with Mukanda the leopard mother searched all over for her little babies, who were in a cage at the back. She flicked open the door of the cage, picked them up ever so gently by her teeth and headed back to the forest.

Next day, when the witch doctor and elders came to get Mukanda for the naming ceremony, they found his hut door swinging open. There was no sound from within, only the rustle of trees out in the wild dark forest.

Kishore's Guardian Angel

A legend from India

Chapter 1

The marriage

A rich corn merchant, known as Lalaji, had an only son whom he adored.

His little Kishore was allowed to play with the sacks full of millet, corn and maize that filled Lalaji's grain shop. Kishore loved to run his fingers through his father's goods. His favourite game was weighing the different grains on the big black iron weighing scales. He couldn't understand why a bagful of maize weighed the same as two bagfuls of fine white flour!

His father explained it to him. 'Quantity is different from weight. You could weigh two babies, but both together might weigh the same as one Kishore!'

Watching his rosy-cheeked boy running in and out of the store room, Lalaji's heart swelled with pride and joy. As he looked at him he thought, 'Why don't I arrange a marriage for my little son now? My best friend Panditji's youngest daughter, Lila, is a lovely little girl. She and Kishore will make such a sweet couple. When they are older they can live together and both our families will be joined forever in prosperity and affection.'

Lalaji was very pleased with his idea and so was his wife. So the following month, when the family astrologer had calculated the best time for the wedding, little Kishore and Lila were married.

In those days, child marriages were common all over India. The husband and wife continued to live with their own parents. Then later, when they were in their late teens, they would share the same home and become man and wife.

Chapter 2
The warning

Kishore finished his schooling and started working in his father's shop. But later, when Lalaji and his wife died, few people remembered that Kishore had been married when he was a small boy.

One day, Kishore's ancient aunt brought it up. She said, 'Kishore my boy, why don't you go and fetch Lila from her parents' house? It's high time you took up your responsibilities as a married man.'

Kishore was very surprised to hear that he had a wife. He had been too young to remember the marriage day.

He asked his servants to arrange a horse and cart, called an *ikka*. He planned to travel to the place where Lila lived and bring her back with him.

He was very excited at the thought of setting up his own home and getting to know his wife.

The cart was a neat small carriage, high off the ground and drawn by a lively black pony. Off they set for Lila's village, but only a few miles on the way a sleek black cat streaked across the track. Black cats are supposed to bring bad luck, so Kishore turned the ikka round and went back home.

The next day, Kishore set off for Lila's village again, but the same thing happened at the same place. A black cat crossed his path and he decided not to continue the journey. They say that when your mind is uneasy and fastens on something, then it is God's way of telling you to pay attention to the matter in hand.

On his third attempt, Kishore saw a very good-looking woman waiting at the place where the cat had been. She held up her hand and signalled for him to stop.

'Oh Kishore,' she said. (He was surprised that she knew his name.) 'Take me with you. You will need me when you get to Lila's house.'

Kishore was puzzled. He was also nervous about allowing a strange woman to travel with him. But, as it was a short journey, he said yes, and the beautiful young woman jumped up beside him.

When they arrived at Lila's house, the woman turned to Kishore.

'Leave me here, but do be careful,' she warned.

'Do not eat the food alone. Eat it with your brother-in-law. If by any chance he is not there, then feed the first mouthful to a dog. Also, be sure to only drink water drawn by your own hand. Whatever else, do not accept even a sip of water from anyone.'

Kishore nodded and said goodbye to the woman.

Chapter 3
Murder!

When they got over their surprise, Lila's family was overjoyed to see their daughter's husband. In India it is not polite for the parents of the girl to send her to her married home without an invitation from the groom's family. They will wait for the husband to come and fetch his wife. So, as they had been waiting quite some time, there was much rejoicing.

But Lila was not as pleased as her parents and relations. She had fallen in love with someone else. Her boyfriend was a policeman and she rushed to him to tell him what had happened.

'Don't worry,' said the policeman. 'Take this little bottle of poison and put a little in your husband's food or drink. He will fall down dead and then you and I can get married.'

Lila hid the poison in her pocket and waited for a chance to feed it to Kishore. To her annoyance her younger brother sat down and ate his dinner with her husband. She could not poison her brother, so she held back.

Just before Kishore went to bed he felt thirsty, so he asked for a glass of water. Here was wicked Lila's chance! While Kishore was in the bathroom, she slipped a few drops of poison into a glass of water and put it beside his bed.

Kishore was sharing the bedroom with Lila's younger brother. Now as soon as Lila left the room, her brother woke up with a raging thirst.

'How lucky', he thought. 'Here is a glass of water just by my bed!' He grabbed the glass and gulped it down. Instead of feeling refreshed he felt sick. He was gripped with a terrible pain in his stomach, and with a cry, he suddenly dropped down dead. The poison meant for Kishore had killed him!

Lila raised a great hue and cry all over the house. 'Kishore has poisoned my little brother! He is a murderer! Call the police!' She was hoping that her policeman boyfriend would arrest Kishore and lock him up. Poor Kishore protested that he was innocent, but Lila pointed an accusing finger at him.

In the middle of all the grief and confusion there was a knock at the front door. A strange woman stood there. She had beautiful slanting green eyes. It was the woman whom Kishore had brought in his ikka.

There was something powerful and mysterious about the woman as she stood in her graceful sari looking at the scene.

'Kishore has done nothing wrong. The young boy was killed by mistake.' She picked up the glass, which still held a little water, and she dropped a fly in it. The fly buzzed round and round, thrashing in the water, and died.

'This water was poisoned by Lila,' announced the woman. 'Ask her where she got the poison from,' she said to Lila's parents. With that she beckoned to Kishore. 'It is time for you to go back home. Leave these people to sort out their business and do not worry about them.'

Extremely shocked, Kishore hastily got his pony and hitched it to the ikka. The woman hopped on again and they rode off into the night.

When they got to the place where Kishore had first stopped for her, the woman signalled that she wanted to get down. With a lithe leap and a bound she was gone from the ikka. Kishore was startled to see her move so quickly. He hadn't even had time to thank her properly.

He looked around but she had disappeared.

All he could see was a sleek black cat, jumping into some bushes.

Kishore's guardian angel had done her good deed and saved him from a terrible fate. He never saw her again.

The Selkie

A folk tale from Scotland

There was once a pretty fisherman's daughter, Ellen, who would go at ebb-tide to gather whelks and other shellfish for the evening meal. She lived near the Old Man of Hoy, a dark rocky stack which leaned out to sea, at a strange angle.

The wind blew and the sea mist swirled round the rocks as Ellen hunted for her dinner. Far off, in the dim twilight, she made out the shapes of seals diving in the sea and returning home for the night.

When she was back in the cottage, Ellen boiled a kettle of water for cooking the whelks and washed some seaweed to make kelp bread. She took the meal to her old father, who was sitting in his rush chair gazing into the peat fire.

'Tell me about the selkies, Father. Is it true that they take off their soft grey sealskin and become human? And is it true that many people have lost their heart to a selkie?'

'There's nothing more to add,' wheezed her old father. 'You know what every Orkney child knows. The selkies are a race unlike man or beast, somewhere in-between. They love us humans, but they also fear us; and in the end they prefer their own. But there's some that say that selkies are the lost souls, the damned, who come ashore in human form just once a year. Others say they are the fairy-folk.'

Ellen thought that she would love to meet a selkie. In the Orkney islands many people believed they had seen selkies, but she was not one of them.

* * *

One day in the springtime, Ellen went out to enjoy the sunshine. The wind was blowing from the south and the snowdrops were pushing up through the turf outside the cottage. She wore a red woollen scarf around her fair hair and pinned up her striped apron to keep it from getting wet.

Ellen scrambled among the slithery black rocks and splashed in pools until she reached the shoreline. The sun was a dazzling yellow, so she shaded her eyes to look out to sea. A whole school of seals was gambolling in the water, throwing off the sparkling drops as they played with one another.

One of the seals bobbed his head in her direction and swam to shore. He came close to the Old Man of Hoy and then disappeared. Ellen scanned the landscape but he was nowhere to be seen.

The sun was hot, so Ellen took off her red headscarf and shook out her long hair. All at once a stranger was standing close to her; a fair-haired man so handsome that she thought she would faint.

'Your hair is so beautiful that I would like to touch it,' he said. Ellen allowed him to feel her silken golden hair. Then she allowed him to hold her hand. Finally she allowed him to kiss her. She was sure that at last she was with the selkie she'd dreamed of meeting one day.

Ellen introduced the young man to her father. He was suspicious of the stranger, but he could see she was deeply in love. He agreed to let them marry.

* * *

Ellen and the Selkie lived with her old father and they were very happy. The Selkie was a great fisherman. He caught enough for them to eat and to sell and so they wanted for nothing.

One day Ellen found she was carrying a baby. When it was born, she was delighted to have a bonny boy. The child was good as gold and so handsome that Ellen could hardly bear to let him out of sight. But her husband, the Selkie, was becoming restless and she knew that he was getting ready to go back to his own people.

One day he kissed her for the last time and said he was feeling the pull of the depths. He was going back to live with the seals. 'I will come back one day. Meanwhile take care of my son for me, for he is the fruit of our love.'

Ellen and the baby went with the Selkie to the rocks where they had first met. Ellen gave her husband a golden chain as a token of her love for him. They watched him go round the Old Man of Hoy as a handsome man. Then they saw him come round the other side as a grey seal with limpid human eyes. With a last nod and a splash he disappeared into the water.

Ellen and her baby boy had each other, but they sorely missed his father. When Ellen's old father died they felt very alone.

She never gave up hoping that her Selkie would come back one day to her, but years went by and he didn't appear.

Then one day, when she was walking with the boy along the shore, she heard singing:

I am a man upon the land, I am a Selkie upon the sea,
And when I'm far and frae from land, my home it is in Skuleskerry.

Ellen knew that the Selkie was coming to her. And he did, bringing with him another precious golden chain for his son.

Once again he left Ellen, but told her that the boy belonged to him and he would fetch him one day soon.

Ellen was heartbroken, but she hugged her son to her chest and prayed he'd never forget her.

She learned to accept that he would leave for his father's home one day.

When that day came, Ellen packed some oatcakes for her boy and pulled a knitted cap of blue wool over his ears. 'Go with your father my son, and think of me sometimes.' She kissed him fondly and let him go with the heaviest of hearts and many tears.

* * *

After many years a good man in the village asked Ellen to marry him. She knew that her beloved Selkie would never come back, so she agreed.

Her new husband was also a good fisherman and brought back full nets night after night. He and Ellen prospered, became rich and had many children.

Then, one night before Christmas, her Orkney husband brought in a great catch. 'It's so heavy that it feels like a crock of gold coins!' he exclaimed.

He opened the nets in the yard and spilled the heavy load of silver fish on to the ground. Among them were two dead seals, and around their necks were golden chains.

Ellen let out a loud cry and fell on the seals. Her Selkie and her son had come home at long last.

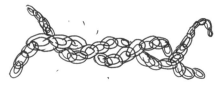

The Golden Apples

A folk tale from Slovenia

Chapter 1

The curse

The King of Bohemia was gazing across his lands from an attic window in his castle. He could see far and wide as his castle sat at the top of a steep crag by the side of Lake Bled.

In the middle of the wide sweep of water was an island where a new church was being built. The King could see tiny, ant-like figures working on the church steeple. Far below, to his right, he took in a green patchwork of fields and orchards. It was all his. The whole, glorious kingdom of Bohemia was his!

On his left he glimpsed the stables and heard his youngest daughter's laughter. She was feeding her pony.

He guessed that her two sisters were looking after their hens and chickens. Meanwhile, their blessed mother (God rest her soul) was peacefully asleep in her grave under the pine trees.

The sun inched higher over Lake Bled. Time was getting on. The girls were growing older and if their mother had been alive, they would have been married by now.

'I should not wait,' the King murmured. 'I need to find good husbands for my daughters.'

After a little more thought he called for the butler, who knew all about arranging parties and balls. 'Start planning the grandest ball we have ever seen in the kingdom. Draw up a guest list of the most suitable princes and nobles. I want my daughters to choose their own husbands. None of this arranged marriage business in our kingdom of Bohemia! We are much too modern for anything like that!'

The butler, whose grandfather had come from Turkey, and whose name was Mehmet, bowed to the King. He started writing invitations to four hundred eligible bachelors who lived near and far.

* * *

• *Mehmet:* (say) 'meh-mat'.   **99**

Mehmet's arrangements were superb. The great hall was hung with wreaths and garlands of cherry blossom. Baskets of pomegranates painted with gold leaf stood in corners. Wax tapers like fat stalagmites cast a soft glow. A long table groaned under the weight of venison, honey cakes and oranges.

Mehmet had invited bands of musicians from every country: drummers from Africa, lute players from Greece, singers from Bulgaria and bagpipers from Scotland.

The great castle by Lake Bled pulsed with light and the sound of music, dancing and laughter.

And what of the three Princesses?

Rose, the eldest, wore a gown of the softest pink. Lily was dressed in white and green satin and Posy, the youngest, looked like a water nymph in aquamarine blue.

The three girls danced all night at their party. Every one of the four hundred bachelors fell in love with one or other of the sisters.

Late in the evening the King of Bohemia clapped his hands for silence.

'Dear guests, the time has come when my beloved daughters are going to go round examining you, talking to you and making up their minds. As you are aware, we are very modern in my country.

'Our girls choose their own husbands. They can, alas, only choose three gallants, so the other three hundred and ninety-seven fine young men are bound to be disappointed. We apologise in advance and would like to thank you for your trouble in coming all this way.

'For my three future sons-in-law I offer a warm welcome in advance. I promise them that I shall not lose three daughters; in fact I shall gain three sons!'

The King made his way to the centre of the hall. 'Now if you could all get into tidy lines – like that – facing the throne, Rose, Lily and Posy will come and inspect you.'

Mehmet took charge. He made sure that all the handsome young men lined up in orderly rows. He showed them how to stand, with their right feet turned out and their hands behind their backs. They might have looked as though they were about to dance the gavotte, but their hearts were thumping in their chests. The young men nervously waited their turn to be sized up.

The sisters tripped down the rows. A few times they caught the eye of a good-looking youth – it seemed they might even stop for a few words with him. But no such luck for the poor young man!

Rose, Lily and Posy, as bright-eyed and smiling as spring flowers, passed up and down all four hundred suitors. Not once did they stop and sigh, or fall in love!

After an hour of this their father enquired, 'Well, my dears?'

'Oh, no, Papa, Your Majesty, we couldn't!'

'Couldn't? Couldn't what?'

'We couldn't possibly go away and leave Ginger the pony ...'

'Or Daisy, Lulu, Natasha or Miro ...'

'Ginger, Daisy, Natasha, and what was he called? Miro? Who on earth are they?'

'Why the pony and the chickens, of course! We can't leave them and go off to some strange place with a strange man.'

The King was appalled at the thought of having to explain that his daughters were rejecting four hundred handsome young men who had come for their hand in marriage.

How could he convey the message without causing deep offence? It might lead to four hundred wars!

'Come, come girls. You don't mean this. Surely you're joking?'

The girls looked at him solemnly with their three sets of beautiful blue eyes. 'Oh no, Papa, Your Majesty, we mean it,' they whispered.

The King struck his forehead in alarm. 'What am I going to tell Mehmet? After all the trouble he's gone to,' hissed the King angrily.

The girls turned around and from a distance blew Mehmet kisses. He smiled and bowed.

'All right then, but I am very disappointed and very ashamed,' and the King once more clapped his hands for silence.

'Ahem, excuse me,' he began.

Four hundred faces turned to him, expectantly.

'I'm so sorry, but there has been a change of plan. Princess Rose, Princess Lily and Princess Posy feel they are still not ready for marriage; they will not be choosing husbands tonight.' He bravely faced everyone, his chin up.

A buzz went through the crowd. It started as a soft buzz and grew into an angry buzz, which then swelled into a roar with a few boos thrown in here and there.

'Unfair!'

'Disgraceful!'

The King held up his hands. 'Have some more to drink and eat, my noble lords. Do try the puddings! Music, music!'

Mehmet looked thunderstruck. All that work for nothing.

Suddenly one of the suitors sprang into action. He struck his crystal glass for attention and his face was dark with anger.

'Your Majesty – this is intolerable,' declared the young lord. 'I came here hoping to find a bride, and I am being sent off with my tail between my legs! I cannot let this pass.

'Your girls need to be punished. In fact you *all* need to be punished for wasting our time. You *will* be punished, your family and all your court. I am not talking here about war, but magic. I have the power to cast a spell on you, but before that I want the other three hundred and ninety-nine disappointed young men to leave. I have no wish to harm them.

'What I am about to do will cause distress to everyone here, so they had better go home.'

Before he had even finished his sentence, the other suitors were hastily gathering their cloaks and belongings and rushing out of the great hall. With a great clattering of swords and belts and dancing shoes, the hall was empty in minutes.

Everyone had recognised Aldred, the great magician. He was famous for his terrible temper and his horrible spells. No one wanted to be caught up in what was sure to follow.

Once the hall was completely empty of guests, Aldred the magician produced his wand from inside his cloak and waved it over the courtiers and the royal family.

The King was wringing his hands saying, 'Do something, someone.' The girls were clinging to one another and the rest of the court, except Mehmet (who was much too proud), were cowering under tables.

Aldred spoke:

'Insults and shame begone begone,
Turn the court of Boheme to stone!'

Instantly, all present company (apart from Aldred of course) froze on the spot. Not a single sign of warm, breathing life remained in the hall.

The King, the Princesses, Mehmet and the entire court of Bohemia became locked in the past; there was no future anymore for them – only a frozen present. They had been turned into stone.

Chapter 2

The three tasks

On the little island that rose from the middle of Lake Bled, the church steeple grew higher and higher. The stonemasons who worked on it were the best in the land. They were three brothers – Todor, Zoran and Silvester (or Silvy for short).

From the top of the steeple, Silvy had a good view of the castle. He was hoping to catch a glimpse of Princess Posy because they had played together when they were young. But he saw no sign of life. It looked as though no one had ever lived there.

Wisps of early morning mist drifted round the gardens, but there was no sound of chickens clucking, nor the pony snorting. Even they had turned to statues of stone.

In the evening, when the three brothers walked back home through town, they saw people gossiping on street corners. They were talking about the events of the ball and the tragedy that had happened afterwards.

An old woman shuffled towards them.

'A crust of bread, my sons?' she begged. Todor and Zoran ignored her and walked on. Silvy who was the youngest, and kindest, offered her the loaf of black rye he was taking home for dinner.

'Bless you, kind sir!' cried the old lady. 'I can see from your gentle face that you are a special young man. May I ask if you are married? Do you have a sweetheart?'

Silvy blushed and laughed. 'No, granny. I am too poor to have a wife. I did once love a beautiful girl – but her family was too grand ...'

The old woman's eyes twinkled. 'Then fate shall give you a fair and lovely princess who will love you. Princess Posy was turned to stone by Aldred the magician. If you can sprinkle her with some special apple juice, she will come back to life. Of course you must do the same for the King and her sisters as well.

After that you will be accepted by her in marriage and never be poor again.'

Silvy could hardly believe his ears. To marry Princess Posy was his dearest wish. 'But where will I find the special apple juice?' asked Silvy.

The old lady whispered in Silvy's ear. 'In the Land of Giants you will find some golden apples. Use these to make the juice. You will have to work long and hard but success will be yours in the end. Take your brothers with you, and when the going is difficult, rub this little stone.' She gave Silvy a small black stone. 'Keep it in your pocket and let it overcome any obstacle that stands in your way.'

Silvy told his brothers what the old lady had said. They were only too ready to go with him and try their luck in the Land of Giants.

At first their father refused to allow them to leave home and their work on the church steeple; but after they pleaded with him all night, he finally gave them permission to seek their fortune.

* * *

The three brothers set off on the long and difficult journey to the Land of the Giants. Each carried a stick with a spotted handkerchief. Inside the handkerchief there was bread, cheese and a juicy green apple.

They walked fast and sang songs. After three days and nights of walking they reached the Land of Giants.

It was a mountainous land covered with thick forests. The giants had curly, long beards and their king lived on top of a steep hill, just like the King of Bohemia.

When the brothers asked him for some golden apples, the King of Giants bellowed at them. 'Do you think this is a charity? The apples and their juice are more precious even than gold or silver! You will have to earn the right to take a basket of apples to Bohemia by completing three tasks.

'For the first task you must climb the Glass Mountain and kill the dragon that lives inside it. The dragon demands a sacrifice every year of a young child. I don't know how many young children we have lost over the years! If you can rid us of this beast, all the people will love you forever.'

Silvy, Todor and Zoran hired three horses and

set off on a gallop to the Glass Mountain, which was a day's ride. They saw it from afar. The sun made it dazzle, so the riders were almost blinded. Then they saw the dragon's breath going up like smoke from an enormous chimney.

When they reached the bottom of the mountain, it was dark. Now the dragon's breath carried sparks that flew up into the night air. They heard its rasping breath, like the wheels of an enormous cart.

Zoran, the eldest, was in despair. 'How will we ever kill this terrible creature? We don't even have a sword between us!'

'Aha, but I have a magic stone!' Silvy took out the little black stone from his pocket and showed it to his brothers.

Todor sneered. 'What? This pebble is going to slay a dragon that eats children? I always said you were a dreamer!'

'Just watch,' Silvy told him, although he had no idea what to do next.

What could he do with the stone? Rub it, spin

it, stand on it or breathe on it? Before he actually did anything, he had to first be clear in his mind what he wanted to bring about. He thought, 'I wish for peace in the Land of Giants. I wish that no more children should be eaten by the dragon.'

Shutting his eyes and sending out his thoughts, Silvy breathed on the stone. Nothing happened.

He rubbed it with his finger and suddenly there was the most terrifying roar from the mountain of glass. It was so loud that the sound cracked the glass itself. With the second roar, the glass mountain shattered into pieces and the brothers saw the dragon writhing and twisting in agony.

In a little while the beast was still. No more breath emerged from its hideous nostrils.

Todor and Zoran had run for cover in some bushes, but as the air became calmer they came out. 'Well done, brother!' They clapped Silvy on his shoulder. 'Let's take back some proof to the King of Giants.'

Treading carefully, they walked into what was left of the mountain, and plucked a spiny hair from the body of the dragon. They stored it in a saddlebag. Then, once they had enjoyed a good night's sleep, the brothers mounted their horses and returned to the Land of Giants.

* * *

The next task was more difficult. The King of Giants had a great lake that flooded during heavy rainfall. Every year the floods destroyed nearby crops and houses. 'You must stop these floods,' demanded the King of Giants. The brothers were shocked – surely this was an impossible task?

Silvy was determined not to be beaten, though. He went to the lake shore and thought hard. He closed his eyes and a picture came into his mind. The picture showed a channel cut from the lake to a nearby river. 'That's it!' he thought. 'When the lake gets full, water can flow into the river instead of flooding over the land.'

Silvy rubbed the stone with his finger. Before

his eyes, a dry canal sank into the ground that led from the lake to the river. Soon the water started flowing towards the river and shoals of fish swam down the canal making the water alive with silvery bodies, moving and twisting towards their new home.

Todor and Zoran had never believed that Silvy could carry out the King of Giant's wishes. They had had a glass of water and gone to sleep in the shade. When they woke up they were overjoyed. They beamed and shook their brother's hand until it nearly dropped off.

* * *

The final task was to create a forest of beautiful trees that would always be full of singing birds. 'Day and night, mind! I want to hear birdsong twenty four hours,' warned the King.

This time Silvy wished for a forest of chestnut, beech, acacia, walnut and wild cherry trees.

He thought, 'Let it be full of nightingales,

warblers, robins and wrens. Let it be home to all the singing birds in this part of the world.' He also wished for the King to be blessed with peaceful sleep, lulled by the beautiful singing of the birds.

Todor and Zoran watched to see what was going to happen. Minutes after making the wish, a forest grew up in the land beside the King's castle. Immediately there could be heard the most glorious mixture of birdsong. It was like a symphony and the King of Giants came out of his castle to listen. He was carrying a basket of gold coloured apples.

He presented the basket to Silvy and wished him well. 'Whatever it is you want, it will always be yours. The juice of these apples can bring life to what has no life. Go and heal the people who need to be made well!'

Chapter 3

New life

With hope in their hearts, Silvy, Todor and Zoran travelled for three days back home, to the Kingdom of Bohemia.

They intended to spend one night at a cottage in the woods, so they knocked on the door and a woman answered. She was sobbing and crying for her dead son. He had fallen out of a walnut tree and broken his head. She had laid him out in the front room.

Silvy immediately squeezed a golden apple and sprinkled the juice on the boy. The lad opened his eyes and got up, completely well and alive.

His mother was beside herself with joy. 'I will prepare a feast for you, kind sirs. You must stay another night!'

But in the middle of the night, Zoran and Todor, unable to sleep, picked up the bag of apples from their brother's bedside and stole away.

They couldn't wait any longer to get to the castle to wake up the Princesses. As they were leaving the cottage Todor returned to leave two apples for Silvy.

* * *

In the castle everything was just as it had been on the night of the curse. A few cobwebs had draped themselves over the statues of the three Princesses.

A robin had made a nest in the King's beard, but otherwise nothing had changed.

Zoran and Todor quickly squeezed the apples to make the juice and sprinkled it over all the court. Everyone started to open their eyes and stretch their arms.

Princess Lily rubbed her eyes. 'Goodness, what a mess after the ball! Mehmet, you'll arrange to get it all cleared up, won't you?'

Rose straightened her pink dress. 'Oh dear, I must go and change my clothes. I think I have a lunch appointment today.'

The King took a few steps. 'Where is my breakfast?'

Everyone was alive again! Everyone except Princess Posy. By the time Zoran and Todor had reached her there was no more juice left in the jug. So she slept on alone, a beautiful but cold stone statue.

Silvy came running up the hill to the castle. He searched for Posy among the bustling court but there was no sign of her. His brothers explained what had happened and showed him where she was. Silvy took the two apples from his pocket, squeezed them and sprinkled Posy with the juice.

Posy yawned and stretched her arms.

'My, that was a lovely long sleep! Rose, Lily,

have you fed Ginger yet? He must be starving. We've danced all night and forgotten about our pets!'

She noticed the three young stonemasons standing in a corner and smiled. 'Have we met before?'

Silvy stepped forward. 'Hello Posy, don't you remember us?'

Posy looked from one brother to another, then back at Silvy. 'Of course! Didn't we play together as children?' Her sisters gathered around, astonished to find their childhood friends now grown into such handsome, kind young men. The same thought flashed into each of their minds. Here were their future husbands.

Posy took Silvy's hand. 'Will you marry me?'

Lily asked Todor, 'And will you marry me?'

Rose did a little dance around Zoran. 'I would love to be your wife!'

And that is how Aldred's terrible spell was broken.

* * *

The King of Bohemia called Mehmet. 'I am sorry to trouble you so soon after that marvellous ball. Could you arrange another party straightaway please? A wedding feast? Just a small affair – only a thousand guests or so. All the royalty of Europe, of course, and every single person in our kingdom is invited.'

'With pleasure, Your Majesty!' And Mehmet went off to make the necessary arrangements. Silvy, being Silvy, forgave his brothers for the trick they had played, and so they all lived happily ever after.